sorry. Sorry, thanks." He huffed, catching his breath.

Peter saw an empty seat toward the front, right next to a girl. When she noticed Peter looking at the space, she slid her book bag onto it.

Peter moved on.

M.J. was sitting next to her friend, Flash.

As Peter walked by their seat, Flash stuck his foot out. *Crash!* Peter tripped and landed on his face.

M.J. gave Flash a look.

"What?" Flash asked.

CHAPTER 2

Later that day, Peter and his science class visited Columbia University.

The teacher hurried everyone into the science building. "Step inside, people!" he said.

A car pulled up to the curb, and everyone turned to look.

Seventeen-year-old Harry Osborn got out of his dad's car.

Harry spotted his friend Peter right away. Peter was hard to miss. As the school newspaper's photographer, Peter was rarely seen without his camera.

"Hiya, Harry," said Peter.

"Hey, Peter," said Harry.

Harry's dad stepped out of the car.

"Peter, this is my father, Norman Osborn," said Harry.

"It's an honor to meet you," said Peter. He shook Mr. Osborn's hand.

Osborn smiled. "Harry tells me you're quite the science whiz."

"Well, I don't know about that," said Peter.

"He's being modest," said Harry. "He wins all the competitions."

"Your parents must be proud," Osborn said.

"I live with my aunt and uncle. They're proud," said Peter.

"What about your folks?" asked Osborn.

Peter put his head down. "My parents died when I was little," he said.

"Hey, you two. I'm closing the door!" yelled their teacher.

"Nice to meet you, Mr. Osborn," said Peter.

Peter and Harry ran up the steps and into the building.

7

CHAPTER 3

Peter, Harry, and the rest of their class-mates filed into the Columbia University Genetic Research Institute. The lab was huge. Microscopes with dials and knobs filled one entire wall. Large cages held spiders of all shapes and sizes.

A tour guide in a white lab coat talked to the class. "All spiders are carnivorous. Arachnids possess different traits that help them in their constant search for food. For example, the jumping spider can leap up to forty times its body length."

Peter asked if he could take a few pictures.

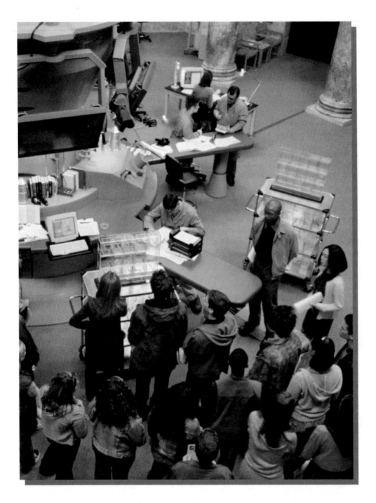

"It's for the school paper," he explained.

The tour guide nodded.

Peter raised his camera. Behind him, one

of Flash's friends bumped Peter's elbow. The picture was ruined.

The guide continued, "The funnel web spider—one of the deadliest spiders in the world—spins an intricate, funnel-shaped web whose strands are as strong proportionally as high-tension wire used in building bridges.

"The crab spider doesn't spin a web to catch its prey, but hunts instead. It has an early awareness of danger, a special 'spider sense,' if you will."

CHAPTER 4

The class was led into another room of the lab. Researchers worked at a ring of computers. Large video screens showed images of spider DNA.

"Over the course of five years, this lab has fully mapped the genetic codes of each of these spiders," explained the tour guide.

The class looked at the spiders. Meanwhile, above their heads, a lone, mutant spider sat at the center of an intricate web.

"We have now begun what was once thought impossible—interspecies genetic transmutation," said the tour guide.

Creepy-looking spiders crawled inside glass tanks. Finally, something interesting!

"Just imagine—if we could isolate the strengths, powers, and immunities in human beings and *transfer* that DNA code among ourselves, all known diseases could be wiped out! Of course, we're not ready to start experimenting with humans, so for the moment, we're working with these fifteen spiders," the tour guide said.

"Fourteen," M.J. whispered.

"Fourteen?" asked Harry.

"There are only fourteen spiders," said M.J.

The missing fifteenth spider hung from the ceiling of the lab. It was busy spinning a new thread. It began to drop down.

The group followed the tour guide into the next room. Peter stayed behind to take more pictures.

The spider continued to make his way down from the ceiling. It dropped onto Peter's right hand—and bit it.

"Ow!" yelled Peter. He shook his hand and the spider fell to the ground.

Peter glanced down at his hand. Two tiny red marks were starting to swell.

Rubbing his hand, Peter ran to catch up with the rest of his class.

CHAPTER 5

Peter's uncle Ben and his aunt May were at home. Ben was changing a lightbulb. He stood on a chair, struggling to reach the ceiling.

Suddenly the front door opened. Peter stumbled in. His hair was tousled, and his eyes were swollen.

"Just in time for dinner," said May.

"How was the field trip?" asked Ben.

"Don't feel well," muttered Peter. "Gonna go to sleep."

"You won't have a bite?" asked May.

"No thanks," said Peter. "I had a bite."

"Did you take some good pictures, Peter?" asked Ben.

"Gotta crash. Everything is fine," he said. Peter staggered upstairs to his room. He slammed the door shut behind him.

"What's that all about?" asked Ben.

"He's a teenager," said May.

Peter was in agony. He dropped onto his knees and clutched his stomach. "Help!" he gasped, but no one heard him.

He fell to the floor, writhing in pain. He raised his hand to look at it. The spot where

the spider bit him was red and more swollen than before.

Peter broke into a sweat. Pretty soon, he was drenched. He started to shake. His face became pale. His teeth chattered. Finally, he passed out. Under his lids, his eyes fluttered.

CHAPTER 6

The next morning sunlight streamed through Peter's window, waking him. He was still lying on his floor where he had collapsed the night before.

He stood up slowly and stretched his legs. He seemed okay.

He glanced at his alarm clock. It was almost eight o'clock. He was going to be late again!

Peter grabbed his glasses, and put them on. He walked right into a chair, and stumbled to the floor. He got up, and put his glasses on again. Everything was fuzzy. He took his

glasses off, and everything was clear and crisp. He put them on and took them off again. He could see better without the glasses!

"Weird," said Peter.

He shrugged, and slipped off his T-shirt. He walked past the mirror, but then jumped back in front of it, and screamed. He had huge muscles!

There was a knock on his bedroom door.

"Peter? Are you all right?" asked his aunt May.

"Fine! I'm just fine!" said Peter.

"Any better this morning?"

"Yes! Yes, much better!" he answered.

Peter threw on a clean shirt and left his room.

He bounded down the steps and leaped over the banister. He landed behind Uncle Ben and walked into the kitchen. Breakfast was on the table. Peter gobbled up the food, and grabbed his backpack.

"Hi. Gotta go!" he said.

"We thought you were sick," said Ben.

"I was. I got better," said Peter.

"Sit down, dear," said May.

"Can't. See you later," said Peter.

He ran out the door.

"What was that about?" asked May.

"He ate my bacon," said Ben.

CHAPTER 7

As Peter stepped out the front door, the school bus drove by. Peter ran to the bus stop, but he was too late. Once more, he started to chase the bus.

But today was different. Peter ran at top speed and easily caught up to the bus. He reached out to the side, and tried to bang on the bus to signal to the driver to stop. His hand slapped a "Go Wildcats!" banner that was pinned to the side of the bus. As the bus accelerated, the banner tore right off.

Peter looked at his hand. He tried to peel the banner off of it, but it was stuck.

Peter's thoughts were interrupted by a loud horn. A huge truck was barreling down the street! Peter screamed. The truck screeched to a halt and the driver frantically jumped out. He was sure he had hit the young man standing in the street.

But Peter was nowhere in sight.

In a split second, Peter had leaped out of the way and on to the side of a building. He was stuck there. He looked down at the sidewalk below. Terrified, he reached for a drainpipe to hold on to. The metal crunched under his grip, and Peter fell.

He landed on the sidewalk. He checked himself, but there wasn't a scratch on him.

A woman leaning out the building window had seen everything. She and Peter locked eyes for a second. Then she slammed the window shut.

Peter ran all the way to school.

CHAPTER 8

Peter's stomach started growling in the middle of his first class. He had never been so hungry. At lunch, he piled his tray with food.

Peter sat down alone in the cafeteria. M.J. moved past him, on her way to her group of friends. As she walked by, she slipped.

At lightning speed, Peter jumped in front of her. He caught her tray with his right hand, and lowered his right shoulder so that she could grab onto it. She regained her balance, and looked at Peter wide-eyed.

"Wow! Great reflexes," said M.J. "Thanks."

"No problem," said Peter.

Peter sat back down. He stuffed his lunch into his mouth. When he was done, he went to put his fork down, but he couldn't. Peter's fork was stuck to his hand!

He tried to pull it free with his other hand, but a long strand of goop stretched from his hand to his fork. Peter tried to separate the fork from the strand. But that didn't work either.

Suddenly a strand shot out from his other hand. This one went flying to the table across from him. It landed on a girl's tray.

Peter looked at the strand. He stood up and tried to back away. He whipped his arm back, and tried to pull free. But instead he yanked the girl's tray off the table. It went flying toward Peter. He ducked as it sailed over his head.

When the strand came free, Peter smiled with relief. He turned around and saw where the tray had landed. It was at M.J.'s table. The flying lunch had spilled all over Flash.

M.J. was covering her mouth, trying not to laugh.

Flash looked around. His eyes darted to Peter. "Parker!" he yelled.

Shocked, Peter turned and ran from the cafeteria.

CHAPTER 9

Peter bolted from the cafeteria, and stopped next to a row of lockers. He sneaked a look at the undersides of his wrists.

He noticed two almost invisible slits in his skin, one on each wrist. He pulled his sleeves down as far as they would go.

A strange feeling came over Peter. Everything around him slowed to a crawl and he had 360-degree vision. He didn't know it at the time, but this was his first experience with spider sense!

He saw Flash's fist—coming toward the back of his head.

Peter whipped around and darted to the side. Flash's fist smashed into the locker.

"Think you're pretty funny, don't you, freak?" said Flash.

"It was an accident," said M.J.

"It really was," said Peter. "I'm sorry."

"My fist breaking your teeth—that's the accident," growled Flash.

A crowd started to form around them.

Flash took two more swings, but Peter was able to avoid them easily. Flash was puzzled. He had been bullying Peter for as long as he could remember. Why were things suddenly different?

Peter sensed danger behind him. He ducked. One of Flash's buddies, who had been sneaking up behind him, was left grabbing air. Peter flipped the guy onto his back.

Harry joined the crowd.

Flash lunged at Peter in a rage. Peter dodged four punches without even moving his feet.

Harry was impressed.

"Harry, please help him," pleaded M.J.

"Which one?" asked Harry.

Flash lunged at Peter again. This time, Peter threw a punch. It landed solidly on Flash's jaw. He was sent flying back against the lockers. He slumped to the floor, out cold.

One of Flash's friends stared at Peter. "You knocked him out!"

Peter gasped. He couldn't believe his own strength.

CHAPTER 10

Peter wanted to test out his newfound powers. He ducked into an alley where he noticed a large, intricate spiderweb between a Dumpster and an alley wall.

Peter approached the wall and examined his hands. Tiny hairs sprouted from his fingertips. He touched the wall and his hand stuck there. He placed his other hand on the wall. It stuck too. Slowly, Peter began to walk *up* the wall. His hands clung like suction cups.

But that wasn't all that Peter could do.

Peter leaped over alleyways, from rooftop to rooftop.

He reached the edge of one rooftop and peered at the one across from it. It seemed too far to clear.

Peter looked down at his wrist. He fingered the narrow slit. Remembering the spiders in the lab, he smiled. Peter turned toward the building across the way and pointed his wrist.

Nothing happened.

He wriggled his wrist, hoping that goop would come out. Still, nothing happened. He tried making a fist, but that didn't work. He rotated his thumb and pinkie together. Nothing. He moved his palm and extended

it, so that all five fingers and his palm were facing upward. He brought his ring and middle fingers together, then lifted them towards his palm.

Thwip!

A single strand of webbing shot out from his wrist. It went straight up and landed nowhere near the building. Peter frowned. This time, he tried to aim the strand. The webbing flew across the alley and stuck to the side of the other building.

Peter tugged on it. It seemed pretty strong. He pulled harder. He was pretty sure it wouldn't break. He wrapped his fingers around the web, closed his eyes, and muttered a small prayer.

Then he jumped off the roof!

He sailed through the air and landed on the side of the other building.

Splat!

He clung there with his hands and feet. His face was smushed against the brick. Okay, it worked. But he needed some practice.

CHAPTER 11

Peter sat in his bedroom that night, flipping through the newspaper. An ad caught his eye.

ATTENTION AMATEUR WRESTLERS! THREE THOUSAND DOLLARS FOR JUST THREE MINUTES IN THE RING! COLORFUL CHARACTERS A MUST!

Peter smiled and ripped the ad from the paper.

He needed a costume. Peter picked up his sketchpad and drew an outline of a human figure. He drew some antennae on the figure. That didn't look right. He ripped out the page.

He drew another figure and stared at it. He sketched some weblike lines over the face

and arms. He drew eyes like large, jack-o'-lantern ovals, with upturned edges.

Satisfied, he smiled at the sketch. This was more like it.

Once he was happy with his costume, Peter needed to figure out how to control his web strands. He set up some empty bottles on a bookshelf at one end of his room. He aimed his wrist at one of the bottles, and put his middle and ring fingers together.

Splat!

A web strand shot out toward the bottles. But it missed them all by a few feet.

Peter fired again. *Splat!* Still, he was nowhere near his target.

Aunt May knocked on his door. "Peter, what's going on in there?"

Peter opened up his door a crack, and peeked out. "Exercising . . . Not dressed, Aunt May."

"Well, don't catch cold," said May.

Peter closed the door and got back to work. A few minutes later, he was still missing his target, and his room was covered with webs.

Peter looked around and sighed.

CHAPTER 12

Peter continued to practice web shooting in his room.

He turned in his chair, aimed his wrist at a can across the room, and fired.

Splat! He scored a direct hit!

He smiled. Next, he aimed at a ceramic lamp. He hit that, too. He yanked the lamp toward him—it came flying across the room. He ducked, and it hit the wall and shattered.

He spun again and fired a double-barreled blast at two bottles. Both strands hit the bottles, dead center. He sent the bottles flying against the wall, where they shattered.

Peter was thrilled. Suddenly there was a pounding on the wall.

"What are you doing in there?" yelled his uncle Ben.

"Studying!" yelled Peter. "Hard!

CHAPTER 13

Peter raced down the steps, his backpack slung over one shoulder. "Going to the downtown library. See you later," he said to his aunt and uncle.

"Hold on. I'll drive you," said Ben.

"It's okay. I'll take the train," said Peter.

Uncle Ben stood up. He grabbed his jacket and keys. "I said I'll drive you. Get in the car."

Peter walked out with Ben following him.

"Thanks for the ride," said Peter when they pulled up to the library.

"Hold on a minute. We need to talk," said Ben.

"Not a lecture, Uncle Ben. I've really got to go," said Peter.

"Aunt May and I don't know who you are anymore. I wonder if you know who you are. Starting fights in school," said Ben.

"I didn't start that fight," said Peter.

"Something is happening to you. You're changing," said Ben.

"How would you know?" said Peter.

"Because when I was your age, I went through the exact same thing," said Ben.

Peter thought about the spider bite, his improved vision, his new strength, and the web strands. He smirked. "Not exactly," he said. "I have to go."

"These are the years when a man becomes the man he's going to be for the rest of his life. Just be careful who you change into," said Ben. "You're feeling this great power, and with great power comes great responsibility."

Peter was getting impatient. "What are you

afraid I'll do, become a criminal? Stop worrying about me, okay? Something is different. I'll figure it out. Stop lecturing me," he said.

He opened the door, and started to get out.

"I know I'm not your father, Peter," said Ben.

"Then stop pretending to be," said Peter.

"I'll pick you up here at ten," said Ben.

"I'm sorry," Peter called out. He wished he hadn't been so harsh with Uncle Ben.

Peter turned and walked up the library steps. When Ben's Oldsmobile pulled out into traffic, Peter turned around and ran down the steps. He ran in the opposite direction. As he moved, he pulled a brown paper bag out of his backpack.

CHAPTER 14

The wrestling arena was teeming with people. All eyes were glued on the center stage. Bone Saw McGraw, a hulking wrestler, was in the process of pulverizing a new victim. Bone Saw grabbed the poor guy, lifted him over his head, and chucked him into the crowd.

The crowd cheered.

"Are you ready for more?" asked the announcer.

The crowd roared.

Bone Saw sat on a stool in his corner. He was sponged off, given water, and massaged.

Bone Saw stood up and flexed. "Bone Saw is ready!" he yelled.

"If the next victim can withstand just three minutes in the cage with Bone Saw McGraw," yelled the announcer, "the sum of three

thousand dollars will be paid to . . ." The announcer stood behind a curtain on the ramp leading to the ring. He covered the microphone with one hand, and turned to the costumed figure next to him. "The Human Spider? That's it? That's the best you got?" he asked.

"Yeah," said the new challenger.

The ring announcer huffed. "You've got to jazz it up a little." He turned back to the microphone. "The sum of three thousand dollars will be paid to the terrifying, the deadly, the Amazing Spider-Man!"

The curtain opened. Spotlights focused on the top of the ramp.

Someone gave Peter a shove. He stepped out and looked around at the arena. The crowd's roar was deafening. He cautiously made his way to the ring.

The crowd started chanting, "Cage! Cage! Cage!"

Cage? What were they talking about? Peter soon found out.

A huge cage was lowered from the ceiling.

The sides fit perfectly over the ring. "Will the guards please lock the cage doors," said the announcer.

Some stagehands came out to wrap huge metal chains around the corners of the cage. Peter and Bone Saw were locked in.

"Hey, wait a minute," said Peter.

Peter turned around. Bone Saw stood in the center of the ring.

"You're going nowhere. I've got you for three minutes of playtime with Bone Saw!"

Peter flattened himself against the bars. "What am I doing here?" he muttered.

Peter leaped out of the way when Bone Saw rushed at him. Bone Saw crashed into the cage wall. He bounced off and crumpled to the ground. He looked up. Peter was clinging to the top of the cage.

The crowd was shocked.

"What do you think you're doing?" asked Bone Saw.

"Staying away from you for three minutes," said Peter.

Bone Saw was furious. He leaped up. Peter

jumped across the cage, somersaulting to the other side. He clung there for a few seconds, and then dropped to the ground.

"Yeah! Go Spider-Man!" cheered the crowd.

Peter turned around. Now the crowd was on his side!

Bone Saw lunged at Peter again. But Peter was faster. He leaped out of the way and did a one-handed handstand on Bone Saw's head.

Peter grinned down at Bone Saw. "Not a bad costume. What is that? Spandex? I used Lycra for mine and it itches like crazy."

Bone Saw took a swat at Peter. He grabbed his leg. "I got you now, insect," he growled. Bone Saw thrashed him around and pitched him against the cage.

"Ow!" yelled Peter.

Bone Saw dragged him to another corner.

"You know, technically, it's *arachnid*," Peter said.

A shadow fell upon Peter. He looked up and saw Bone Saw flying at him with his elbow jutted out. Peter flipped his feet up just in time. They made contact with Bone Saw's chest and kicked him into the far wall of the cage.

The crowd started chanting, "Spider-Man! Spider-Man! Spider-Man!"

Peter looked around the arena. He raised his arms in triumph. "Ah, showbiz," he said.

CHAPTER 15

After the fight, Peter went up to the arena office to collect his prize. His mind was racing with the thought of the three thousand dollars. He had never had so much money.

The promoter handed him a hundred-dollar bill. "Now get out of here!" he yelled.

"A hundred bucks? The ad said three thousand dollars."

"Check it again, web-head. It said three grand for three minutes. You pinned him in two. For that, I'll give you a hundred, and you're lucky to get it. You made my best fighter look

like a mouse out there," growled the promoter.

"I need that money," Peter said.

"I missed the part where this is my problem," said the promoter with a smirk.

Peter stared at him. Burning with rage, he turned to leave. He passed a squirrelly looking guy with platinum-blond hair on his way out.

Peter walked down the corridor, clutching the lousy hundred-dollar bill. He was almost at the elevator when he heard a shout from behind him.

"Hey, what do you think you're doing?" yelled the promoter.

Peter turned to look. The door to the promoter's office banged open. The squirrelly looking guy raced out, clutching a canvas bag.

"Help! That guy's got my money!" yelled the promoter.

The bell of the elevator behind Peter dinged. The doors opened, and the thief took off down the hallway toward it.

Peter looked at the thief racing toward him. He thought about it for a minute. He was still

mad about the three grand. He took a step back.

The thief raced right past him, into the elevator. "Thanks, pal," he said.

The doors closed, and the squirrelly looking guy got away.

The promoter came rushing out of his office. "You let that guy get away with my money!" he yelled.

Peter shrugged. "I missed the part where this is my problem," he said. He turned on his heel, and walked away.

CHAPTER 16

Peter walked down the street toward the public library. He was in his street clothes again. He looked around for Uncle Ben's car. He looked left and right. Uncle Ben was nowhere in sight.

A police car raced by with its siren wailing. Peter decided to check out the scene.

Suddenly he had a bad feeling. He walked faster. Then he broke into a run.

In the middle of a large crowd, the police were standing over a body.

"Uncle Ben!" yelled Peter.

"Hang on, hang on," said one cop.

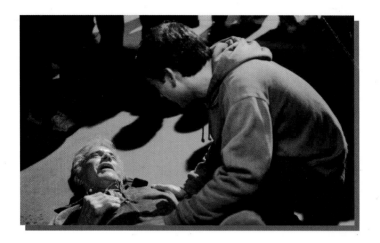

"What happened?" asked Peter.

"It was a carjacker. He's been shot," said the first cop.

Peter pushed past the cops and kneeled in front of his uncle. He took his head in his lap.

"Uncle Ben! It's me, Peter!" he yelled.

Ben's eyes fluttered open weakly. His mouth formed a thin smile. "Peter," he whispered. Then he died.

Peter hugged his uncle and wailed.

A third cop spoke into the radio. "They got the shooter! He's headed south on Fifth Avenue."

Peter listened intently.

CHAPTER 17

In a dark alley, Peter tore off his clothes to reveal his Spider-Man costume. He started to run. He jumped up on the side of a building and clung to it. Then he started to climb.

He jumped backward and grabbed hold of a flagpole. He swung on it, allowing his momentum to hurl him to the next building. He climbed to the top.

He stood at the ledge and peered over. He saw the police cars screaming down Fifth Avenue in pursuit of the carjacker.

Thwip!

A silver strand of web fluid shot out across

the street. Spider-Man wrapped his fingers around it and leaped.

He swung across the city as the car chase continued directly below him.

Down on the street, Ben's Oldsmobile went screeching around a corner. Three police cars followed.

Above, Spider-Man swung from his webs, unseen.

He swooped down and landed on top of the Oldsmobile.

His fist slammed through the roof. He grabbed hold of the carjacker's face.

Gunshots erupted through the roof of the car. Spider-Man was fast enough to dodge the bullets. But he had to leap off the car and onto a speeding truck. He stood up, eyes focused on the Oldsmobile.

The truck headed toward a low bridge that stretched straight across the street. Spider-Man did a triple somersault, up, over the bridge, and landed on the roof of the truck again.

Spider-Man jumped back onto the roof of

the Oldsmobile. He smashed his fist through the windshield, and shot out some webbing.

The carjacker was blinded. The Oldsmobile swerved out of control. It smashed through the gates of an old building, with Spider-Man clinging to its hood.

The car screeched toward the front door. Spider-Man had to leap off to keep from being crushed. He crawled out of sight.

The police cars arrived seconds later.

CHAPTER 18

The carjacker cowered with his gun in a far corner of the building. The police shined a bright beam around the room.

Spider-Man descended, upside-down, from a web strand. He rotated, and landed softly on his feet, right next to the carjacker.

The thief whirled around and fired shots at Spider-Man. Spider-Man leaped onto the nearest wall and clung to it.

The carjacker kept blasting shots at him. But Spider-Man leaped from wall to ceiling to wall to floor—inches ahead of the bullets.

Spider-Man did an acrobatic leap and

landed on the carjacker's arm. He kicked the gun free. It skittered across the cement floor.

Spider-Man lifted the guy up and made a fist.

"This is for the man you killed!" he yelled.

He punched the carjacker in the face. The carjacker sailed into one of the windows.

The carjacker spoke. "Don't hurt me! Give me a chance."

"Did you give him a chance? The man you killed? Did you? Answer me!" replied Spider-Man.

Spider-Man looked down at the carjacker. He held him in a sliver of light, so he could see the man's face.

A sick feeling washed over Spider-Man. He was the squirrelly man with platinum-blond hair—the thief who had stolen the money at the arena, the one Spider-Man had let get away.

"No! No, not you!" moaned Spider-Man.

Spider-Man hurled the carjacker across the room. The truth was too awful to accept. Peter had failed to stop the very man who had murdered his uncle.

Peter was devastated. The thief scrambled for his gun and stood up. He was just ten feet away from Peter. He aimed the gun at him and pulled the trigger—the gun was empty.

The thief backed up further. He crashed through a window. Peter lunged forward to catch him, but he missed.

The thief fell fifty feet and smashed onto the dock below, dead.

CHAPTER 19

Outside, the police shined a spotlight into the window. Peter was peeking out at them.

"There's the other one!" shouted a cop. "I told you there were two of them."

Peter disappeared from sight.

A dozen cops smashed through the door. They shined their flashlights in every corner. The building was empty.

Peter was sitting on a rooftop. He was still in his spider suit, but he was not wearing the mask. He dropped his head in his hands.

"Uncle Ben," he whispered. Tears ran down his face. "I'm so sorry."

Hours later, Peter went home. His aunt was waiting up for him. He told her the tragic news and tried to comfort her.

CHAPTER 20

It was graduation day. High-school students in caps and gowns swarmed all over the school lawn.

"We made it, buddy," Peter said.

"Good news," said Harry. "My father owns a building downtown with an empty loft. He said I could live in it. Why not move in with me?"

Peter smiled. "I've got to get a job first."

Harry saw his father with Aunt May and jogged over to him. He held his diploma in his hand. "Hey, Dad," Harry said.

Mr. Osborn looked at his son proudly.

"You made it. Congratulations."

"Thanks," said Harry.

"Congratulations, Harry," said May.

Aunt May gave Peter a hug. "Here's our graduate," she said. "You two looked so handsome up there."

Mr. Osborn put his arm around Peter. "I know this has been a hard time for you, but try to enjoy this day."

"Thanks, Mr. Osborn," said Peter.

He missed his uncle very much.

CHAPTER 21

Aunt May and Peter went back to their house in Queens.

Peter carried his cap and gown up the stairs.

Aunt May held his diploma. "Can I fix you something to eat?" she asked.

"No, thanks," said Peter. He went into his room and sat on the side of his bed.

A minute later, May appeared at his door.

She put his diploma on his desk and sat down next to Peter. She put her hand on his shoulder.

"I missed him a lot today," said Peter.

"I know. I miss him, too." May took his

hand. "But he was there."

"I just wish I hadn't—" started Peter.

"Peter, don't start that again." May sighed.

"He tried to tell me something important and I threw it in his face," said Peter.

"You loved him and he loved you. He never doubted what kind of man you will grow into. How you are destined to do great things. You won't disappoint him. Or me," said May.

She squeezed his hand and stood up. May left the room, quietly closing the door on her way out.

Peter got up and opened his dresser drawer. His Spider-Man costume was crumpled in a

corner. He traced the spider outline with his finger.

He heard Uncle Ben's voice in his head. "With great power comes great responsibility," it said.

Peter looked at the Spider-Man costume. The task ahead would be difficult. But Peter knew what he had to do. After all, he was Spider-Man.

COLUMBIA PICTURES PRESENTS A MARVEL ENTERPRISES PRODUCTION A LAURA ZISKIN PRODUCTION "SPIDER-MAN"
STARRING TOBEY MAGUIRE WILLEM DAFOE KIRSTEN DUNST JAMES FRANCO CLIFF ROBERTSON ROSEMARY HARRIS
MUSIC BY DANNY ELFMAN EXECUTIVE PRODUCERS AVI ARAD STAN LEE SCREENPLAY BY DAVID KOEPP BASED ON THE MARVEL COMIC BOOK BY STAN LEE PRODUCED BY LAURA ZISKIN IAN BRYCE DIRECTED BY SAM RAIMI

MARVEL

sony.com/Spider-Man

COLUMBIA
PICTURES

Spider-Man®: Spider Bite
Spider-Man, the character, ™ and © 2002 Marvel Characters, Inc.
Spider-Man, the movie, © 2002 Columbia Pictures Industries, Inc. All rights reserved.
Photography by Zade Rosenthal
All photographs © 2002 Columbia Pictures Industries, Inc. All rights reserved.

First published in the USA by Avon Books in 2002
First published in Great Britain by
HarperCollins*Entertainment* in 2002

HarperCollins*Entertainment* is an imprint of
HarperCollins*Publishers* Ltd, 77-85 Fulham Palace Road,
Hammersmith, London W6 8JB

The HarperCollins website address is
www.**fire**and**water**.com

1 3 5 7 9 8 6 4 2
ISBN 0 00 713799 0

Printed and bound in Great Britain by Scotprint

Conditions of Sale

GO FOR THE ULTIMATE SPIN AT
www.sony.com/Spider-Man

Spider Bite

Adapted by Leslie Goldman

Based on the screenplay by David Koepp

Photography by Zade Rosenthal

■ HarperCollins*Entertainment*
An Imprint of HarperCollins*Publishers*

CHAPTER 1

Peter Parker was late again. He ran to the sidewalk just as his school bus was pulling away.

The bus sped down the street in Queens, New York. Peter lowered his head and started to run.

His classmates looked out the windows and laughed at him.

M.J., Peter's neighbor, asked the driver to stop the bus. "He's been chasing us since Woodhaven Boulevard," she said.

The bus driver slowed the bus to a stop. Peter caught up to it and climbed in. "Thanks,

PROLOGUE

Who am I?
You sure you want to know?

Mine is a tale of pain and sorrow. And that just covers the high-school years.

I've warned you that it isn't pretty, but you asked for it. So here it is—the story of how I became Spider-Man.

3